SPIDERS IN THE HAIRDO

Spiders in the Hairdo

Modern Urban Legends

collected and retold by
David Holt & Bill Mooney

August House Publishers, Inc.
LITTLE ROCK

Published 1999 by August House, Inc.,
P.O. Box 3223, Little Rock, Arkansas, 72203,
501-372-5450.

Printed in the United States of America

10 9 8 7 6 5 4 3

LIBRARY OF CONGRESS
CATALOGING-IN-PUBLICATION DATA
Holt, David.
Spiders in the hairdo : modern urban legends /
collected and retold by David Holt & Bill Mooney.
p. cm.
Includes bibliographical references.
ISBN 0-87483-525-9 (tpb. : alk. paper)
1. Urban folklore—United States.
2. Legends—United States.
3. United States—Social life and customs.
I. Mooney, William. II. Title.
GR105.H63 1999
398.2'0973'091732—dc21   99-11973

Executive editor: Liz Parkhurst
Illustrations by Kevin Pope
Book design by Patrick McKelvey
and Katrina Kelso, AdManInc.

The paper used in this publication meets the
minimum requirements of the American National
Standard for Information Sciences—Permanence of
Paper for Printed Library Materials, ANSI Z39.48-1984.

AUGUST HOUSE   PUBLISHERS   LITTLE ROCK

Contents

Introduction

"A family purchased some fried chicken at a fast food place. One piece was really tough. When they looked closely they realized it was a Southern-fried rat."

"In New York City, kids bought baby alligators for pets. When the fad wore off, they flushed them down the toilet. Now those alligators are full-grown monsters living in the sewer system."

Have you ever heard stories like these? They are *urban legends* —our modern-day folktales. More accurately called *contemporary legends* (because "urban" implies a city setting that doesn't always characterize such legends), these tales, heard in conversations, found in newspapers or television and radio newscasts, are always reported as true. Occasionally, they even emerge as plots for television shows.

These contemporary legends can be found in many variations all over the world. Usually, they are passed on through conversation, the settings and characters changed to reflect the attitudes and societies of the teller and the listener.

Invariably, these stories are never told by the person they supposedly happened to; rather, they have happened to a friend of a friend (the teller's aunt's neighbor, boss's daughter, etc.). For this reason, some scholars call these legends *FOAFtales*— because they always happen to a Friend Of A Friend. The person telling such a tale honestly believes it is true and that a first-person account lies just a few informants back. Each story sports just enough credibility to make it plausible.

Webster's Ninth New Collegiate Dictionary defines a legend as "a story coming down from the past; *esp.:* one popularly regarded as historical though not verifiable." We don't often think of a legend or folktale as occurring in the present, but urban legends are part of our modern-day folklore. Unlike older, more fanciful folktales, contemporary urban legends concern recent events or situations that could be real. In keeping with our modern sensibilities, they are usually full of irony and occasionally have a supernatural element. Modern urban legends reflect our concerns, our fears, our prejudices, and our delight in other people's folly and misfortune. In short, they tell us a lot about ourselves.

Contemporary legends are usually told in conversation as anecdotes or short short stories—rarely full-length tales. The story "Losing in Las Vegas"—often referred to as "The Stolen Kidney"—might be told in conversation something like this: "Did you hear about that guy who was in Las Vegas and went with some girl back to her hotel room? Next thing he knew, he woke up in a strange room and discovered one of his kidneys had been removed. There's a crime ring that's stealing them and selling them overseas ..."

Most often, just the bare bones of the story are related, but, as with any intriguing tale, the plot can be expanded and embellished to suit the teller and the audience. As long as the essential core is included in the telling, the stories work.

Contemporary legends are extremely effective in the classroom. Young people—especially teenagers—love them. Whether you live in the city or the country, these legends are relatively easy to come by. Students can collect them from friends, family, books—even the Internet. Using this book as an example, they can find variants of contemporary legends in their area and expand the essential core of the tales to fully realized stories. Given a sure-fire plot, students learn what it takes to flesh out a simple narrative and invest it with a sense of place and character.

You are holding in your hands a collection of our favorite contemporary legends. We have kept the tone of a few of them anecdotal—as they might be heard in conversation—but we have expanded most of the legends into full stories. The simple yet bizarre plot twists of urban legends are wonderful material for the modern storyteller. We have expanded the characters and settings of the original anecdotes, sometimes combining several story threads, as you will discover when you read "The Hook" and "The Deadly Dress."

This has been our goal throughout—to flesh out the bare bones of the contemporary legends to entertain you, the reader. If you are looking for a more scholarly approach, refer to the books listed in Further Resources.

Some of the tales are really gruesome, even downright gross. Nobody knows where they come from. But remember, we didn't make up the plots of these tales. You did—or, at least, other people like you did. Some, like "The Vanishing Hitchhiker," have been around for centuries and keep being dressed in new clothes. (The hitchhiker legend has even been seen recently on television commercials, clad in designer jeans.) Ever-changing, they continue to reflect some part of who we are.

We all have a need to tell stories. It has been said that stories are our native language. Whether for education or entertainment or edification, we have been telling stories since our ancestors first hunkered down around a campfire. Stories capture our imagination and allow us to clearly visualize and remember information.

Today we are inundated with narratives from movies, television, newspapers, and novels; yet, we still enjoy hearing a good tale told by a friend. In these hi-tech times, the old folktales have been relegated to storytelling festivals, library programs, or children's bedtime. They are rarely told informally among friends. Into that void steps the "new" urban legend. Because they are incredible yet believable, such legends satisfy our ancient need to hear and tell stories.

It is possible that some of the magic of these stories will eventually be lost. More and more people know what an urban legend is and are sophisticated enough to identify and debunk them. Part of the reason the tales are so enjoyable is because most people still think they are true. Without this element of "truth," urban legends could go the way of old jokes, lurking forgotten on the sidelines of society until they are rediscovered.

But then again, maybe not. We have heard from several sources that the stolen kidney legend mentioned earlier has become so widespread the Las Vegas Chamber of Commerce has undertaken a publicity campaign to calm travelers' fears and to assure them that the story is unfounded, untrue, and merely a part of urban legend lore.

We phoned the Las Vegas Chamber of Commerce to find out if this was, in fact, true. They reported to us that no such public relations campaign ever existed, nor was there one in the works. So here we have a new urban legend growing out of an older one. You just can't hold a good story down.

With our irrepressible need for stories and the treasure trove of weirdness in the modern world, it is a safe bet that we humans will keep creating and believing new urban legends as long as we exist.

We hope you enjoy these urban legends. And keep your ears open for new ones, for they are born every day.

—David Holt and Bill Mooney

Fools Rush In

35 m.p.h.

A lawyer, driving along the freeway in his brand-new BMW, was on his way to a very important appointment. Lost in thought about his strategy for the meeting, he was brought back to reality when his car suddenly stalled. He coasted over to the side of the road and tried unsuccessfully to get the car started again. His repeated efforts only exhausted the battery.

Upset about being late for the meeting, he got out of the car and started waving his arms, hoping to flag down someone who would stop and help. Presently, a sixteen-year-old boy, armed with his brand-new driver's license, pulled over and backed up. "You need help?" he yelled.

The lawyer told the teenager that all he needed was a push to get his car going.

"It's an automatic, so you have to get up to thirty-five miles an hour for it to do any good, to get the motor turning over. You understand?"

"Sure thing, man. Thirty-five. No problem!"

As the teenager backed up behind him, the lawyer got back in his new Beamer. He sat and waited. And waited. Checking in his rearview mirror to see what the delay was, he gasped.

The boy's car was bearing down on him—going thirty-five miles an hour.

Bringing Home the Bacon

A man was driving through the countryside. As he rounded a long curve, he saw a car coming from the opposite direction. Just as the car passed him, a woman leaned her head out the driver's window and screamed, *"Pig!"*

The man was taken aback. He stuck his head out of the car window. "Yeah?" he retorted. "Well, you're not so good-looking yourself!"

Just as he turned his eyes back to the road ahead, his car slammed into a five-hundred-pound pig.

Shot in the Head

One hot midsummer day, a man was walking through a supermarket parking lot when he noticed a woman slumped over the steering wheel of her car, holding the back of her head. He thought she must be taking a nap. When he returned to his car a little later, he noticed the woman was still in the same position.

Perhaps she's had a heart attack, he thought.

The man opened the car door and said, "Ma'am, are you all right?"

"Please, please, call the doctor," she said, not looking up. "I've been shot in the head and my brains are coming out."

The man looked in the back seat of the car. He saw the ragged end of a cardboard tube that had PILLSBURY printed on it. The heat had caused the tube to explode. The sticky biscuit dough had hit her in the back of the head and was oozing between her fingers.

He leaned in and said, "Ma'am, you're going to be all right. You just need to learn the difference between brains and biscuits."

The Concrete-filled Cadillac

Debbie was a beauty. She turned men's heads no matter where she went, no matter what she was wearing. She was shapely, sweet, and smart. Many men had asked to marry her, but she didn't say yes until she met Norman, a handsome cement contractor. He seemed kind, sensitive, and more attentive than any man she had ever met.

Debbie and Norman were married and lived together happily ... for a while. Soon, however, Norman began to notice that every time he was with Debbie in public, men would turn their heads and stare. The more it happened, the more jealous he became. Often, if he left her side—for instance, to get popcorn at a movie—someone would come over and try to pick her up. Even at church, the minute he moved away from her, men would flirt shamelessly with her. It maddened him that Debbie was so sweet to these men. After all, she was his!

Norman's jealousy grew until at last he convinced himself that Debbie was seeing someone behind his back. He started calling home during the day to see if she was there. On the rare occasions when she wasn't home, she always had a plausible explanation. It drove him crazy that he couldn't catch her being unfaithful to him.

He began driving by their house at various times of day to see if her car was still there or if anybody was visiting her. Sensing his unreasonable jealousy, Debbie simply tried to be sweeter to Norman.

One day, when Norman was driving to a job site with a loaded cement truck, he decided to swing by their house and check on Debbie. As he rounded the corner, he saw, parked at the curb, a shiny red '57 vintage Cadillac convertible. It had a luxurious white leather interior, wood-grain dash, and sleek chrome-trimmed tailfins. He looked at the house and, through the picture window, he saw his wife inside, smiling and talking with a handsome young man, obviously the owner of the swanky Cadillac parked at the curb.

Norman had finally caught her! Rage boiled up inside him.

He wondered how he could get this guy. Then he remembered he was hauling a full load of Lloyd's Quick-Dry Cement. He backed up his truck to the Cadillac and set the brakes. As the big cylinder turned the load of wet cement, Norman positioned the lip of the trough over the Cadillac's leather seats. He pulled a lever and the cement began to flow. Within a minute the Cadillac was filled to the top of the doors. Norman quietly drove away with a great feeling of self-satisfaction.

After work that evening, he strutted into his house wondering how his wife would describe her day. But the house was dark, his dinner wasn't ready, and Debbie was nowhere to be found. He heard crying coming from the living room. He found Debbie lying on a couch, her eyes red, tears rolling down her cheeks. Norman walked up and said cockily, "Well, Debbie darling, how was your day?"

"The most awful day of my life," she sobbed. "I had planned such a wonderful surprise for you. I'd bought you the most beautiful vintage Cadillac. The salesman even brought it here. But while I was signing the papers, some idiot came along and filled it completely with cement. Who would do such a thing?"

Norman never questioned his wife again. He left the cement-filled Cadillac at the curb as a monument to her faithful love and his foolish jealousy.

A group of young boys lived near the railroad tracks. Every day after school they played on the tracks. A favorite game was to put coins on the tracks and wait for the next train to roll over them and mash them flat.

One of the boys was afraid to get close to the railroad tracks. All the other kids called him a wimp.

"I'm not a wimp," he said, "and I can prove it."

"Oh, yeah?" one of the bigger boys said. "Prove it!"

"How?"

"Put your tongue on the track."

"Tongue on the track? Uh ... OK."

They liked that. "OK, but we get to choose the day."

"Fine," said the little boy. "Any day. I don't care."

They waited until January 13th. It was bitter cold.

"OK, wimp," the boys said, "today is the day."

After school, they took him down to the railroad tracks. The little boy cautiously lay down on the ground next to the track. He stuck out his tongue and touched it to the cold steel. In an instant, it froze to the rail. The boys began to laugh.

They had forgotten about the 3:15 train. When they heard the whistle and felt the rumble in the tracks, they started yelling, "Get back! Get your tongue off the track!"

The boy tried, but he couldn't tear his tongue loose. He pulled his head back as far as he could. Just then, the train roared by, cutting off the end of his tongue.

The boy survived, and he learned a valuable lesson. To this day, he still says, "I'll neh oo at agin."

Swept Under the Rug

A carpet layer had just finished installing a new carpet for a wealthy lady. He went outside to smoke and realized he had lost his pack of cigarettes. The workman returned to the living room to look for them and noticed a lump under the carpet. Not wanting to tear up the newly laid carpet for a pack of smokes, he took out his hammer and flattened the bump.

Later in the day, as he was about to leave, the lady of the house called out to him. "Here is your pack of cigarettes I found on the front porch," she said. "Now, could you help find my baby hamster? It seems to have gotten out of its cage."

The Jet Car

The Arizona Highway Patrol found a twisted mass of smoldering metal embedded in the side of a cliff. They speculated that it must be the wreckage of an airplane until they checked closer, finding fragments of a bumper. The car—125 feet up the side of a cliff—was so demolished the police couldn't detect what make or model it was.

After extensive testing, the police lab finally figured out what happened.

A man had obtained a JATO (Jet Assisted Take Off) Unit, used to give extra power to military transport planes on short runways.

The man attached the rocket booster to the top of his 1967 Chevrolet Impala. He found a long straight stretch of road in the desert, lined up his car, and fired up the JATO Unit.

The police could tell by the scorched and melted asphalt three miles from the side of the cliff where the car finally became airborne. They calculated that the rocket reached its maximum thrust in about five seconds. During that time, the car attained a speed of four hundred miles per hour. It stayed on the highway for two and a half miles. The last mile, the driver stomped on the brakes until they melted. The tires blew, leaving thick rubber marks on the road. The Impala finally became airborne, crashing into a cliff 125 feet above the road, leaving a blackened crater three feet deep in the rock.

There was nothing left of the driver but a greasy spot. But what a ride!

The Home Front

Wake Up, Honey!

A pilot who worked for an international airline had just flown in from Singapore. It had been a long, arduous flight. He got home at four A.M. and fell asleep, dog tired. At seven o'clock, his wife came upstairs and shook him.

"Honey, I hate to wake you, but we're having guests tonight and the drain in the sink is completely stopped up. Can you come down and unclog the U-pipe for me?"

The pilot always slept in the nude. Wearily, he got up, slipped on a light bathrobe, not bothering to tie it, and stumbled downstairs. Still groggy from lack of sleep, he got down on all fours, stuck his head underneath the sink, and began unscrewing the U-pipe from the drain.

He didn't know that his wife had just adopted a little kitten. Like all cats, the new kitty was curious and wanted to see what the pilot was doing with his head under the sink. It crawled underneath the man's robe, looked up and saw something dangling above him. Being playful, the kitten swatted at it.

When the pilot felt an attack in such a sensitive place, he jerked his head back, hit the underpart of the sink, and knocked himself out.

His wife came downstairs shortly to find her husband unconscious under the sink. Thinking he had had a heart attack, she called the emergency squad. As they were putting him on the stretcher, the pilot came to and saw his wife holding a kitten. It began to dawn on him what had happened.

When the pilot explained what had happened, the paramedics started laughing so hard they dropped the stretcher and broke his leg.

Cat and Mousse

A young housewife, newly married, was giving her first dinner party. Her husband had invited several people from work, including his boss. It was going to be a very special dinner. She asked her husband what she should serve.

"Oh, serve salmon mousse," he said. "You do that so well."

She purchased the salmon and left it on the kitchen table while she assembled the rest of the ingredients. When she turned around, she saw their cat on the table, nibbling the fish. She chased it away.

"Oh well," she said to herself. "They'll never know the cat ate some of the fish. I'll just wash it off and finish fixing the salmon mousse."

The dinner party was a great success. After the evening came to an end, she began cleaning up. When she took out the garbage, she saw their cat lying by the side of the house—dead. She couldn't imagine what had killed the poor animal. Then she remembered the salmon. It must have been tainted.

She quickly called all the dinner guests, including her husband's boss, and explained what had happened. She urged them to go to the hospital immediately to have their stomachs pumped.

The following morning, her next-door neighbor rang the doorbell. She looked sheepish as she explained to the wife that the evening before, while backing her car up, she had run over their cat. She was so sorry—she had been in a big hurry to pick up her husband, so she just left the cat by the side of the house. Had they found it yet?

The Cupboard Was Bare

Millie's husband had been gone a year, drafted into the army and sent to Korea to fight in the war. On the morning of the anniversary of his departure, she felt especially depressed. She walked upstairs to the bathroom and filled the tub with hot water, hoping that a good soak would help.

As Millie started to get into the tub, it occurred to her that she had neglected to lock her doors. Nude, she padded downstairs and locked the front door; just before she reached the back door, however, she heard someone coming up the steps.

Oh, no, she thought. *It's the milkman!*

Looking for the nearest place to hide, she ran into the pantry and closed the door. She heard a knock at the back door, then another knock. After a moment, she heard a voice say, "Millie? You there? I've just come to get a cup of sugar."

It was her mother-in-law! She lived just a couple of doors away.

The back door opened. Millie heard footsteps approaching the pantry where she was hiding. She saw the pantry door swing open and watched as her mother-in-law gasped in astonishment.

Millie blurted out the first thing that came to mind.

"Sorry, I was expecting the milkman!"

About a week before Christmas, a scrawny little abandoned kitten came to Ruth's door. She took it in, fed it, and decided to keep it. She prepared a litter box and kept the kitten indoors for a few days so it would know this was its new home. On Christmas Eve, Ruth let it out in the front yard for the first time.

Just as the kitten walked down the front steps and started playing in the yard, the neighbor's pit bull ran down the street and started chasing it. To get away, the kitten climbed to the top of the tallest, thinnest tree.

Ruth was furious. "Get out of here!" she yelled at the dog. She then tried to coax the kitten down from the top of the tree.

"Here, kitty, kitty, kitty ... Come on down ... it's all right now ... come on, kitty."

The kitten wouldn't budge.

Ruth could see it was hopeless. When her husband came home, Ruth said, "Honey, get the ladder and see if you can get our little kitten out of the tree."

He brought out a ladder, leaned it against the tree, and climbed to the top rung. Still, he couldn't reach the cat.

"Come on down, kitty. This is your last chance."

The kitten tried to climb higher in the tree.

"I've got an idea," the husband called to his wife. "Get some rope out of the garage and bring the car around to the front of the house."

Ruth backed the car around to the front yard. Her husband tied one end of the rope halfway up the tree and then tied the other end to the bumper of the car.

"OK now, honey," he said. "Drive forward very slowly. One foot on the brake, the other on the gas. The tree will bend down. When it does, I'll grab the kitten."

"You're going to break my beautiful birch tree."

"No," he said. "It's young, it's strong. It'll bend easily. Just drive slowly."

As Ruth inched the car forward, the tree began bending just as her husband had said. The little kitten clutched desperately at the branches. The husband was just about to reach up and grab the cat when the rope broke.

The tree snapped upright, catapulting the kitten out of the tree like a missile. Screeching and windmilling its legs, the kitten flew over their house and the top of the next house. Then it disappeared from view.

Ruth and her husband felt sick. They combed the neighborhood, but couldn't find a trace of their kitten. Sadly, they returned home.

A few days after Christmas, Ruth was in the grocery store. She saw her neighbor, Dorothy, in the pet food section.

"What are you doing buying cat food? I always thought you hated cats."

"The strangest thing happened to me on Christmas Eve," said Dorothy. "I was at home alone, feeling sorry for myself, no one to share Christmas with. I decided to go out back to do a little yard work. It usually makes me feel better. I was raking leaves, praying somebody would come and visit. All of a sudden, I heard a screaming sound. It got louder and louder. I turned around and a cat came flying out of the sky, right over the house, and hit me in the face. It was the cutest little kitten!

"You know I don't like cats, but I decided to keep this one. How could I ignore a sign like that from God? So I named it Angel, because it came from the sky."

*L*ife on the *O*pen *R*oad

An elderly couple were driving their RV to a favorite camping spot, located by a river in a particularly secluded glen. Having been at the wheel for some time, the man became drowsy and asked his wife to take over. He was going to get in the back of the RV and take a nap.

It was a hot day and the air conditioner was not working well, so before the man got into bed, he took off all his clothes so that he would be more comfortable. The traveling motion of the RV soon rocked him to sleep.

As he woke up from his nap, the man felt the RV come to a stop. Still lying in the bed, he looked up and saw trees through the windows of the RV and heard what sounded like rushing water. Delighted that he had slept all the way to the secluded camping spot, the nude man got up from bed, opened the door, and stepped to the ground. Just as he did, the signal light turned green and his wife drove away, leaving the man standing in the middle of a city wearing nothing but a sheepish grin.

A Special Halloween

A young couple received an invitation to a Halloween party that had a reputation for being wild and fun. That evening, however, the wife told her husband that she had had a hard day at work and didn't really feel like going.

"Put on your costume," she said, "and go without me. I'm sure you'll have a good time."

"You know, I think I will," he said. "I feel like partying tonight."

After her husband left, the wife began having second thoughts, wondering how her husband behaved at a party when she wasn't present. *I could put on a different costume and mask,* she thought, *and he wouldn't know who I am. I could watch him and see what he does.*

She donned a costume, wig, and mask that her husband had never seen and drove to the party. She watched her husband dance with other women, flirting with them. When he came over and asked her for a dance, she knew he didn't recognize her. At the end of their third dance, he asked if she would like to go to the bedroom with him.

She followed him to the bed to see how far he would go. She wouldn't let him take off her mask, so he kept his on as well. The mystery of the masks made for an exciting bout of lovemaking.

Afterward, the wife stormed away from the party. Back home, she sat in the living room, waiting for her husband to return. As he walked in, she asked, "How was the party?"

"Oh, it was OK," he said.

"You had fun, didn't you?" she retorted. "Lots of fun!"

"Well," he said, "I guess it was all right. When I arrived, hardly anyone was there. So I went downstairs and played poker with the boys. My brother arrived without a costume, so I let him wear mine. I didn't have much fun, but he told me he had a *great* time!"

The End to a Perfect Meal

Donald, a portly young man, had fallen in love with an equally portly young woman, Jeanine, the daughter of the town's wealthiest family. When he was invited to her house to meet her parents, he wanted to make a good impression. Jeanine told him her mother was preparing a fancy dinner, so Donald was determined to be on his best behavior.

The dinner table glistened with expensive china and crystal. He was seated next to Jeanine's mother. The servants placed course after course of rich, delicious food in front of him. Each dish was better than the last. Donald ate every morsel and did not refuse the offers of seconds and thirds. He had never eaten such wonderful food and could not get enough.

He was careful to make no mistakes in table etiquette. He waited to see which fork or spoon Jeanine's mother used before he picked up his. He kept his free hand in his lap, except when he tipped his soup plate away from himself to scoop up the last scrumptious spoonful, something he had seen Jeanine's mother do. He used his napkin repeatedly and never put his elbows on the table.

Donald felt he was making a good impression. He had answered the family's questions about what he was doing and what he expected to do with the rest of his life. Again and again, they had smiled their approval.

There was only one unpleasant aspect of the evening. He was getting full. His waistband was too tight and made him extremely uncomfortable. His stomach needed more room to expand. As the attention and conversation switched to someone else, Donald reached down and quickly unbuckled his belt.

When that didn't give him the relief he needed, he unbuttoned the waistband. It was still not enough, so to ease his distress, he pulled down the zipper until, at last, his stomach felt comfortable.

Now, with his pants open, Donald confidently began to eat the wonderful dessert, a huge piece of chocolate cake accompanied by a mountain of mocha ice cream.

When the meal was over, Donald reached under the table and, struggling, zipped up his pants and re-buckled his belt. He was effusive as he told Jeanine's parents how much he had enjoyed the evening. Then, as he got up and moved away, everything on the table—the expensive china, silver, crystal—came crashing to the floor.

When he zipped up his pants, he had inadvertently stuck part of the tablecloth in there as well.

He was not invited back.

A Rude Awakening

Finding his wife in the throes of a massive heart attack, an elderly man called the rescue squad. The paramedics arrived promptly but too late to save the old woman's life. After they pronounced her dead, the rescue workers placed her body on a stretcher. As they carried her to the ambulance, they accidently bumped the stretcher against a tree in the front yard, causing the old woman to fall to the ground. The shock of the fall revived her, and she lived.

A couple of years later, the wife had another heart attack. Again, the paramedics arrived too late. They loaded her onto the stretcher and started carrying her out of the house. When they got to the front yard, the husband yelled, "You fellows watch out for that tree!"

The Mexican Pet

A woman who lived in San Diego, California, loved to cross the border to shop in Tijuana, Mexico. One day when she came out of a store in Tijuana, she saw a cute little dog. There were always lots of stray dogs running around Tijuana. It looked to her like a Mexican Hairless.

The woman took pity on the animal and gave it a few bites of food. Then she went into another store. It followed her. When she came out, she petted and fed it again.

The little animal followed her all day. By the time she was ready to drive home, she had fallen in love with it. She thought, *I can't bear to be parted from this cute little thing. I love it so much.*

She knew, however, that U.S. agricultural regulations concerning plants and animals would not allow her to take her new pet directly home. It would have to be quarantined for several months.

The woman piled her purchases in the back seat, put the Mexican Hairless on the seat next to her, and drove north. As she neared the border, she opened a couple of buttons of her blouse, picked up her new pet, put it inside the blouse, and buttoned it up again.

At the border, the agricultural officer asked, "Anything to declare?"

The woman showed him everything she had bought.

"Did you bring back any plants or animals?"

"No, nothing."

"All right, drive on."

After the woman got home, she fed her new pet and made a little bed for it.

When she got up the next morning, she found her Mexican Hairless still in its bed, looking sick, with foam around its snout. She scooped up the animal, bed and all, and rushed to the veterinarian's office. She told the nurse, "Please make my little doggie well."

The nurse picked up the bed and carried it inside. Fifteen seconds later, the vet hurried out and said, "Lady, where did you get this animal?"

"He just showed up at my house the other day. I love him so much. He's such a cute little thing."

"Lady, tell me the truth. Where did you get this animal?"

"I told you he just showed up."

"No, lady, you didn't get this animal in this country. Now, where did you get it?"

"Oh, all right, but don't breathe a word of it to anyone. I was down in Tijuana yesterday and this cute little Mexican Hairless kept following me around and I couldn't bear to be without him. Please make my little doggie well."

"To begin with, lady," the vet said, "this animal isn't a dog, it's a Mexican sewer rat. And it has rabies. You're lucky you got to me before it got to you."

Hot Dog!

A woman had a little pet Yorkie. Since her carpet and furniture were white, the woman insisted that her dog be spotlessly clean. She bathed the Yorkie at the slightest suggestion of dirt. In the wintertime, after she bathed the Yorkie, she would put him in the electric oven to dry.

One Christmas her family gave her a microwave oven. She seldom used it except to thaw frozen food and melt cheese, but she could see that the microwave oven cooked a lot faster.

One particularly cold day, she wanted to dry her little Yorkie a bit quicker than usual so he wouldn't catch cold. She put him in the microwave oven and set the timer for five minutes. When she returned, she found her Yorkie still wet—but cooked from the inside out.

Running for the Phone

A young married couple, living in an apartment in Seattle, owned four big German shepherds. The wife was leaving to visit her mother in a neighboring state, so she told her husband, "The dogs have to be walked at least four times a day for exercise."

"How am I going to do that?" he said. "You know I can't leave the office."

"I don't care how you do it, but find a way."

Just then, the phone rang. The dogs began running through the apartment, barking and leaping until the husband answered the phone.

He had his solution.

The morning after his wife left, he walked the dogs. Before he left for work, he turned off the answering machine. At eleven, he called his apartment, letting the phone ring sixty times. Then he hung up, knowing the dogs had spent the time running around the apartment.

At two o'clock, he phoned his apartment again. That evening, he went home and walked the dogs for real.

He was very proud of his plan and told a colleague at his office what he had done. The next morning, the colleague, who was something of a practical joker, saw the husband's keys lying unattended on his desk. He put them in his pocket, drove over to the apartment, and let himself in. Sure enough, at eleven o'clock, the phone rang and the dogs started running and barking. The practical joker let the phone ring a few times. Then he picked the receiver and began to pant heavily—like a dog that has been running. Then he barked and hung up.

The Old College Try

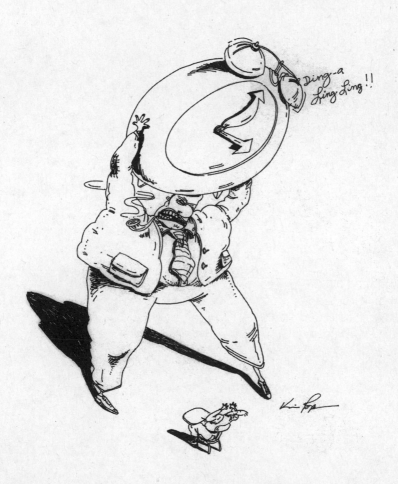

The Blue Book Scam

It was time for final exams at the university. One student, who had partied long and late the night before a psychology final, was afraid he would not do well on the test. As he walked into class, he saw the two blue books the professor always provided for the final, to make sure no one could cheat.

He had no idea how to answer some of the exam questions, so he devised a plan. He began to write a letter to his mother in the first blue book. He told her how he had finished the exam early and had some extra time, that things were going well at the university and how much he liked his psychology professor. He went on to explain that he felt he had done very well on the test and was just killing time until the period was over.

At the end of class, he handed in the blue book that contained the letter to his mother. He then ran to the library, looked up the answers to the exam questions, and wrote them in the second blue book. He sealed it in an envelope and mailed it to his mother.

A couple of days later the professor called him and said, "Why in the world did you turn in a letter to your mother?"

"Oh, I'm so sorry," said the student. "I finished the test early, so I wrote a letter to my mom in the other blue book. I guess I got the two blue books mixed up. Tell you what, I'll call my mother and have her send the letter back to you unopened. It won't even come through me."

When the grades were posted, the student had aced the class with an A.

Do You Know Who I Am?

A college professor had a large lecture class. He was famous for giving difficult tests unannounced. Outside of class, he was known by the students as "The Dread."

The class hadn't had a test for a while and the students were getting nervous that he might surprise them. Near the end of the Thursday class, one of the students asked the professor if there was going to be an examination on Friday.

"You'll see me crawling through the transom over the door before I give a test on Friday and have to grade papers on the weekend," he replied.

The next day, as the students came into class, they were surprised to see blue books on their desks. They heard a rustling sound at the door and turned around to see the professor crawling through the transom. "It's test time!" he yelled.

"The Dread" wrote the test questions on the board and told the class they had exactly one hour to finish. Anyone writing after the test period was over would automatically fail the exam.

Every student wrote furiously until the professor shouted, "Time's up! Put down your pens."

One student kept writing, trying to complete the last question. He finished a minute later and took the blue book up to the professor's desk, where the other student's tests were piled high.

"I'm sorry," said the professor. "You went overtime. You have failed this test."

"Sir!" said the student indignantly. "Do you know who I am?"

"Young man, I have no idea who you are."

"Good!" said the student. Quickly, he jammed his blue book into the middle of the stack and ran out of the classroom.

The Loving but Cold Hand

A newlywed college couple was irked one winter morning when they discovered their car wouldn't start.

"Look, honey," said the husband, "you walk on to class. I'll stay here and work on the car."

When his wife came back a couple of hours later, she saw a pair of legs sticking out from underneath the car. Feeling playful, she scooped up a handful of snow, walked over, unzipped her husband's pants and gave him such a frigid surprise that he jerked up and hit his head on the underside of the car.

She shook him but he wouldn't rouse. When she ran inside to call the ambulance, she found her husband at his desk studying.

"I just couldn't do anything with the car," he said, "so the garage sent over a mechanic. He's working on it right now."

The Pledges' Revenge

It was Bryan's first year at the university. His older brother, Jimmy, was now in medical school at the same university. Jimmy had made it clear that Bryan should pledge the Delts. He considered it the best on campus; its members had more parties and more fun than any other fraternity.

Jimmy didn't know, however, that the pledgemaster at the Delts, Randolph Crabtree, was every pledge's nightmare. Several times a week, Crabtree would awaken the pledges in the middle of the night, herd them into his small upstairs bathroom, and pull the chain to turn on the light. He then forced them into a cold shower with all their clothes on. After they were soaked, he would make them go back to bed, shivering in their wet clothes.

Crabtree forced the pledges to swallow live goldfish and wear baloney insoles in their shoes. At dinner, he would serve them mashed potatoes covered with castor oil gravy. Then for dessert, he would bring out brownies iced with a chocolate-flavored laxative.

The hazing began to drive Bryan crazy. Crabtree had singled him out as his special target. Bryan had become so scared of Crabtree that he had bitten his nails to the nub and was failing his courses. In desperation, Bryan asked his brother what he should do.

"Jimmy," he said, "it's hideous what we're being put through. We need to fix Crabtree and fix him good."

"Give me several days to think about it," Jimmy said.

A week later, Jimmy brought Bryan a package. When Bryan opened it he found, wrapped in tissue paper, a severed human hand. Jimmy told him he had cut it off a cadaver and smuggled it out of his anatomy class.

"Sometime when Crabtree is away from his room," said Jimmy, "tie this severed hand to the pull chain in the bathroom and see what happens."

Saturday night was Crabtree's big party night. The pledges knew that after a few beers, he would be meaner than ever. At eleven o'clock, Bryan sneaked into Crabtree's bathroom and tied the severed hand to the light's pull chain. He quietly closed the door and returned to his room.

The pledges lay in their beds waiting for Crabtree's return. At three in the morning, they heard him stumble up the stairs. He opened the door to their room and yelled, "Hey, frogs! I hope you're not sleeping too tight. You guys need a shower. It stinks in this room." Belching, Crabtree lurched out of the pledges' room.

The pledges got out of their beds in the annex and ran to the window. They could see Crabtree's window across the way. Chuckling under their breath, they waited for the light to go on—and for Crabtree's scream as he clasped the cadaver's hand on the pull chain.

The light came on, but there was no scream. No noise. No Crabtree bursting out of the bathroom. Just silence.

"What's he doing?"

"Maybe he's sneaking down here to throw us in the shower—or worse."

They waited five minutes. Ten minutes. Then they started to get concerned.

"Think he's all right? You know, if he was OK, he'd be down here kicking our tails. Something's wrong."

The pledges went to Crabtree's room. There was no answer when they knocked. They pushed open the door. No Crabtree. The light was on in the bathroom. They looked in. There, crouching in the shower, was Crabtree. His hair was completely white. He had a crazed look in his eye as he sat chewing on the fingernails of the severed hand.

Scary Stories

The Babysitter

Bob and Terri Nixon loved to eat out. Even after they started a family, the Nixons still loved to dine at restaurants several nights each week. They were able to do this only because they had found the perfect babysitter—Mary Lou Farley. She was bright, responsible, and pretty. The Nixons felt fortunate to have Mary Lou look after their two children.

One night, at the last minute, the Nixons called Mary Lou to ask if she could sit for them.

"Sure," she said. "I was studying for a final anyway and then I was just going to watch my favorite sitcom."

The Nixons assured her they would be back by ten-thirty in order for her to get plenty of rest before the test.

Mary Lou came over, played with the kids, fed them, and put them to bed. She studied until nine, when she switched on the television. Not long after she started watching her show, the phone rang. She picked up the receiver.

"Nixons' residence."

At first she heard nothing but loud breathing sounds. Then a voice: "I'm upstairs. I've got the kids, and now I'm waiting for you ..."

More breathing sounds.

Mary Lou put down the receiver, feeling scared. Then she thought, *Wait a minute, it's just a crank call. Maybe the Nixons have been getting a lot of them lately.* She turned her attention back to the sitcom, hoping to lose her fear in its laughter.

Once more the telephone rang.

"Nixons' residence."

Again, she heard heavy breathing. "I'm upstairs," the creepy voice repeated. "I've got the kids, and now I'm waiting for you."

As Mary Lou slammed down the receiver a second time, she realized the Nixons had only one telephone line coming into the house. Nobody could be calling her from upstairs.

What nonsense! she thought. *But maybe, just to be sure, I'd better run up and check on the kids. Wait a minute! What if I'm wrong? What if there really is somebody up there with them?*

As a feeling of terror swept over her, she picked up the phone and dialed 911.

"Emergency."

"Hello, this is Mary Lou Farley. I'm babysitting for the Nixons on Valley Drive and I've just had a couple of really scary calls. The guy says he's upstairs with the kids and for me to come up. It's scaring the socks off me. Could you listen in on this line? I'm sure he'll call back in the next few minutes. Then you could find out where he is and send a patrol car by and make him stop calling me. I'm here by myself."

"All right," said the operator. "We'll put on a tracer. Try to keep the caller on the line as long as you can so that we can find out where it's coming from. In the meantime, we'll send a police cruiser around right away."

As soon as Mary Lou hung up, the phone rang again.

"Yes, hello, Nixons' residence."

"I'm upstairs. I've got the kids, and now I'm waiting for you. What's taking you so long?"

"Who's calling? Who is doing this calling?"

"I told you—I'm upstairs, and I'm waiting for you. Come up and find out who's here."

"Please tell me who you are and where you're calling from."

"I'm calling from upstairs and I've got the kids and I'm waiting for you."

"Please, you're scaring me."

"I'm not trying to scare you."

The phone clicked in her ear.

Mary Lou was terrified. Her first impulse was to run out the front door. But she knew she couldn't leave the kids.

Once more, the telephone rang.

"Yes, yes," said Mary Lou. "What do you want?"

"It's the police. The call is coming from a second line in the same residence where you are now. Get out of the house immediately."

"But what about the children?"

"The cruiser will be there in thirty seconds. Get out of the house now!"

Mary Lou dropped the phone and started running. As she

50

opened the door, she saw the patrol car pull up, its lights flashing. As two cops got out of the cruiser, she ran toward them, screaming, "Upstairs! There's an office upstairs. Mr. Nixon must have put in a fax line. Maybe that's where it's coming from."

The patrolmen ran upstairs. Mary Lou, following them in a panic, saw them apprehend a man climbing out of an open window in the hallway.

"Oh, my God, are the children all right?" she cried.

Mary Lou opened the door to their room and looked in. There, unaware of the commotion, sleeping in their beds, were the two children.

As the police shoved the intruder into the police car, a crooked grin formed on his face. He looked back at Mary Lou, standing on the front porch. She shuddered as she heard him say, "I'll call you later. You can count on it."

The Slasher

*Over the course of five years, we spent a number of weeks each theatrical season touring our musical play, **Banjo Reb and the Blue Ghost**, which we co-wrote and co-starred in. Due to the erratic schedule of the tour, we spent a lot of time in airports. To keep our brains from turning to dust and dribbling out our ears (which happens if you spend too much time in airports), we began to create stories. The following story, one of our first, is not, strictly speaking, an urban legend, although it draws its inspiration from several of them.*

It was a quarter to midnight when Cynthia finally got off work. She and the other two waitresses stood huddled at the back door of the tavern, looking out at the darkened parking lot where their cars were.

They were scared.

They had good reason to be.

There had been eight murders in the county in the past month. All of them had been committed by somebody the newspaper was now calling "the Slasher," for the grisly way that he left his victims.

Cynthia and the other two waitresses agreed that none of them would pull out of the parking lot until they all had their motors running and their headlights on. They looked at each other.

"Are you ready?"

"Yes, ready."

"One, two, three ... go."

The three of them sprinted out into the darkened parking lot. Cynthia opened the door to her car, got in, slammed the door, slapped down the lock button, stuck the key in the ignition, and turned it on. The motor started easily. She reached over and pulled on the headlights.

Looking at the dashboard, she saw the gas gauge was registering empty, the needle hovering at the lower corner of the *E*.

Oh, no, Cynthia thought. *How stupid of me not to get gas this morning before I came to work. There's no place in town to get gas now. Well, I probably have enough to get home. You never know how much gas you have in the tank when the needle is on empty. And, besides, if worse comes to worst, I can always stop at Sam's Country Store on the way home and wake up Sam and have him fill the tank for me. He'll be crabby, but at least he'll do it.*

Cynthia flicked her high beams at the other two waitresses and they all drove off in their separate directions.

Driving home this late at night was always a little scary for Cynthia, because she lived a good ways out of town with her parents. But it was particularly scary tonight with the Slasher on the loose.

These murders, they've always taken place in towns, never out in the country, she thought. *So I'll probably be safe.*

She turned on the radio to keep herself company. It was playing her favorite song, "I Can't Get No Satisfaction." The familiar lyrics made her feel more comfortable.

As she got outside of town, wisps of fog began to roll in over the highway. She flicked on her high beams so she could see down the road a little bit better. There, far, far in the distance, she saw what looked like the figure of a man. He seemed to be waving his arms at her as if he wanted her to slow down.

I wonder if I know him? she thought. *I'd feel so much safer if I had somebody that I know here with me in the front seat. I wonder what he's doing here? Maybe he's had a roadside accident or something.*

As she drove nearer to him, he kept motioning her to slow down, pull over, and stop. As she got closer, she saw he had a long white beard and splotches of red on his white shirt. She also noticed that he had piercing pale blue eyes.

He kept motioning to her to pull over and stop. As she braked, the radio broke into her thoughts.

"This is headline news at midnight. The Slasher has just claimed his ninth victim—Mr. Eli Williams of Jacksonville, Florida. The police report that Williams was able to wound the Slasher quite severely before Williams died of his own wounds. The Slasher is still at large, still armed, and extremely dangerous. If you are driving, do not pick up any hitchhikers. If you are at home, do not open your door to strangers. And report any suspicious behavior to the police."

By this time, Cynthia's car had almost come to a complete stop. The man with the long white beard and the piercing blue eyes was shuffling toward the passenger side of the car. Just as his hand reached for the door handle, Cynthia pressed down hard on the accelerator. Her car fishtailed down the two-lane road.

She looked in the rearview mirror and saw that the man with the long white beard and the wild blue eyes was running down the road after her car. She felt as if she could hear him breathing as he ran.

I can't be expected to pick up anybody, not now, not this time of night. Not with the Slasher on the loose. I mean, for goodness sake, if he is the Slasher, that's a job for the police. And if he's not, if he's had an accident, well ... that's also a job for the police.

She looked along the sides of the road to see if she could spot any houses. She thought maybe she could stop at one of them and phone the police. But there were no houses; she was on a barren stretch of the road.

Her car sped faster and faster, now going 68, 69, 70 miles an hour. She looked down at the gas gauge. The needle was now below the *E. Oh, please,* she thought. *Please give me enough gas to get home. I've got to have enough gas to get home.*

As she rounded a long lazy curve, the fog started to dissipate. She flicked on her high beams.

There, far down the road, she saw the figure of a man walking down the yellow line toward her. As she drove closer, she saw the man had a long white beard.

How'd he get here? What's he doing here? I didn't see any car along the road, and there aren't any side roads along here. How could he possibly get here ahead of me?

As she drove closer, she saw the man motion her to slow down and stop. Her car was now going 74, 75 miles an hour.

When she was directly in front of the man, she pulled the car to the left, gravel spraying from the back wheels. She pulled around him and got back onto the two-lane road, the car fishtailing again.

She looked in the rearview mirror. The man with the long white beard and the piercing blue eyes and the blood matted on his white shirt had turned around and starting running after her again. She felt like she could hear him breathing as he ran. She felt like she could smell the blood on his shirt.

Her car was now going 83, 84, 85 miles an hour. She looked down at the gas gauge. The needle was virtually horizontal. She depressed the accelerator and sped faster down the road.

As she started up the long hill before Sam's Country Store in the valley down below, her car was going 90, 91, 92 miles an hour. When she neared the crest of the hill, she heard her car motor cough ... sputter ... then die.

Cynthia looked down.

Indeed, the needle in the gas gauge was well below empty. She turned the key in the ignition, trying to get a spark from the engine. She began slipping the clutch and the accelerator, hoping to get the motor to turn over again.

The car had been going so fast it still had enough momentum to coast to the crest of the hill. As it started to slowly roll downhill, she looked up and ...

THERE HE WAS!

Right in front of her!

Cynthia closed her eyes and screamed, expecting to hear a loud *whock* as the car hit him.

But she heard nothing.

Moments later, she opened her eyes.

There was nothing in front of her except Sam's Country Store, illuminated by the vapor lamp in the valley down below. She looked in the rearview mirror. The man with the long white beard and the blood all over his shirt and the wild piercing blue eyes had started chasing after her car. He was so close, in fact, she felt like he could reach out and touch the trunk of her car.

"Roll, car, roll!" she screamed.

The car kept picking up more and more momentum as it coasted down the hill, moving faster and faster toward Sam's Country Store in the valley down below.

As she pulled up in front of Sam's and stopped the car, she blew the horn. Then she opened the door, screaming.

"Sam! Sam, wake up! It's me, Cynthia. Wake up, please, Sam!"

She tore open the screen door and started pounding on the wooden door.

"Wake up, Sam, wake up, it's me, Cynthia! Hurry, wake up!"
That's when she saw the note pinned to the front door:

GONE FISHING—BE BACK THURSDAY

Today was Wednesday.
"No, Sam, no."
She turned and looked behind her. The man with the long white beard and blood all over his shirt and wild blue eyes was still running down the hill. He was getting closer and closer. Then Cynthia noticed the phone booth.

She sprinted toward the phone booth, digging in her purse, trying to find a quarter. Why, why had she changed all of her tip money, all her coins, into dollar bills before she left the tavern? How stupid of her.

She got into the phone booth, closed the door, and turned her purse upside down. Out fell her lipstick, her comb, her brush, her keys, and finally, stuck in the lining, a quarter. She turned and looked.

The man with the long white beard and the blood all over him was getting closer and closer. She lifted the coin up to the slot, but she was shaking so badly she fumbled it. The quarter dropped to the floor.

She reached down to try to get the quarter, but the phone booth was too small. She couldn't reach it. She had to open the door. She looked back. The man with the long white beard was getting closer.

She had to chance it. She pulled open the door, reached down, picked up the quarter, slapped the door closed again, braced it with her foot, took the receiver off the hook, and pushed the coin into the slot. She heard the coin fall and then the dial tone. Just as she was about to punch in the numbers, she realized it was too late.

The man was right next to her—his face was pressed up against the glass of the phone booth. She turned and looked at him—his face no more than six inches away.

She dropped the receiver and started screaming. She felt she was watching herself in some kind of horror movie, and while everything else was moving in real time, she was in slow motion.

She watched as the man, blood matted in his beard and shirt, pressed his face up against the glass. His wild piercing blue eyes stared in at her. She watched his mouth, pressed against the glass of the phone booth, tear open and close, tear open and close.

As she watched in horror, she heard sounds coming from the mouth.

"Eezin yurca. Eezin yurca. Cawlapleez!

"Eez in yur car. Eez in yur car. Call a pleez!

"He's in your car. He's in your car. Call the police!"

The next morning, the newspaper headlines read:

SLASHER CAPTURED!
*Found Bleeding to Death
in Back Seat of Local Woman's Car*

Cynthia turned the page of the newspaper and saw a picture of the slasher's ninth and last victim: Mr. Eli Williams of Jacksonville, Florida. It was only then that Cynthia realized who had chased her so relentlessly the night before—who her ghostly savior had really been. There was no mistaking Eli Williams' long white beard and his piercing pale blue eyes.

The Deadly Dress

Beth was excited as the senior prom approached. She had been invited to the dance by the all-star quarterback, Roger McGrath, the most popular boy in the senior class. She couldn't believe her good fortune. Her only concern was finding something beautiful to wear.

Beth knew all the other girls would attend the prom wearing fine, expensive gowns. She also knew her mother wouldn't be able to afford anything like that. Beth lived with her mom—her father had cut out years ago—and had to work at a fast-food restaurant after school to help make ends meet. A fancy new dress was out of the question.

"I have an idea," her mother said. "I know a wonderful secondhand shop where they always have beautiful evening gowns."

The dress that caught Beth's eye was a lovely deep red. It fit her like a second skin, following her every curve, as if it had been made just for her. When she put it on, she felt like a movie star.

Prom night arrived, and Beth looked stunning. Roger told her how proud he was to have her for his date. All the boys wanted to dance with her, but Roger wouldn't give them a chance. Every dance was his.

The gym grew hot and stuffy as the dancing continued. Shortly after midnight, Beth began to feel faint. Her skin had a tingling sensation and her arms and legs started to go numb. She asked Roger to take her outside to get some fresh air, but it didn't help. Finally Roger told her, "I think I better take you home."

By the time they arrived at her house, Beth could hardly walk. "All I want to do is lie down, Roger, just rest awhile. I feel so tired."

Beth's mother thanked Roger for bringing her home.

"I'm sure she's feeling this way because she got over-excited and worn out from the dancing. She'll be all right in the morning."

Beth fell across her bed and went right to sleep. Her mother took off her high heels and pulled the spread over her, not bothering to take off the red dress.

The next morning, when Beth's mother went in to check on her, Beth's skin was chalky and pale. When her mother held her wrist, she felt no pulse. She ran to the phone and dialed 911. Then she phoned the family doctor, who lived just a few doors away.

The doctor was there in a matter of minutes. After examining her, the doctor shook his head. "I'm sorry," he said quietly. "There's nothing more I can do. She's gone." He sent away the rescue squad; then he called the funeral home.

When the funeral director arrived, Beth's mother explained that she had very little money and asked that his services be kept as inexpensive as possible.

"I understand your situation," he said. "We will have a simple service with a dignified plain coffin. Preparations will be kept to a minimum."

Beth was taken to the funeral home and the red dress was removed to prepare her body for burial.

"Don't bother to embalm this one," said the funeral director. "It's a charity case. The viewing is tonight and the burial is in the morning. She's a pretty girl. Just put a little makeup on her and get her back in the red dress. She'll be fine."

At the viewing that night, friends and family came to grieve and pay their respects. After the mourners left, the director closed the lid to Beth's coffin.

Once the funeral home's doors were closed, the cleaning woman started her rounds. The first thing each evening, she looked in the coffins to see if there might be something to steal. It was easy to take jewelry. Sometimes, if she knew the casket was to be buried the next day and wouldn't be reopened, she took the clothing from the body.

When the cleaning woman opened up Beth's coffin, she was surprised to see a beautiful red dress—a dress she had stolen and sold at least twice before. Odd, she thought, that this dress should keep turning up on dead people.

She had always been sorry she had sold the red dress. It looked as if it would fit her perfectly. This time, she decided, she would keep it for herself.

It was a struggle, but she finally got the dress off Beth's body. She then closed the coffin, finished her cleaning, and left.

The next morning, a long procession of high school friends followed the hearse to the cemetery.

As the coffin was being lowered into the ground after the graveside service, a muffled knocking sound was heard coming from it.

"Stop! What's that?" Beth's mother shouted.

The knocking sound was heard again.

"Open up the coffin. Quick, open the coffin!"

The lid was thrown open. There lay Beth—naked but alive, gasping for air.

Her mother pulled her from the coffin and wrapped a blanket around her. After the hysteria died down, Beth said, "I could hear what was going on all around me, but I couldn't move or talk. I was paralyzed. While the undertakers were preparing my body, I could hear them but I couldn't move or say anything. I started to come to once they took my dress off. But then they put it back on and I became paralyzed again. Later, someone took my dress off once more, and slowly, I began to revive. There must be something in that dress. I thought I would never be able to get the strength to move or make a noise. Thank God you heard me before it was too late."

The police were called in. Their first stop was the second-hand store where Beth and her mother had purchased the gown. They asked the owner where the red dress came from.

"Red dress?" he said. "Why? What's the problem?"

"We think the dress is contaminated with a deadly poison ... some sort of embalming solution."

"Embalming solution ... you mean from a corpse?"

"That's right."

"You say it's a form-fitting red dress?"

"That's right, a prom dress."

"Oh, yeah, I remember it. Odd, it's been in and out of here several times. Wait a minute ... I think the woman I bought it from cleans businesses ... maybe even funeral homes. I couldn't tell you her name, though."

It took two days for the police to track down the name and

address of Rosemary Ross. When detectives knocked at her door, a sad-eyed man opened it slowly.

"Excuse us, sir, but this is an emergency. We are looking for Rosemary Ross."

"You're too late," said the sad-eyed man. "A couple of nights ago I took her to a dance. She looked eighteen again. Her hair was done up and she had on a beautiful new dress, but by the end of the evening she was dead. It's hard to believe"

"What color was the dress?" asked the policeman.

"Red. Why?"

"Quick, where is she buried? We need to get a crew out there immediately and dig her up."

"Buried? She wasn't buried. We cremated her this morning."

Billy leaned over to kiss Jennie. He had been dreaming all week about this moment. He had finally talked his father into letting him have the car for the night. Billy and Jennie had driven up Mulholland Drive, overlooking all of Los Angeles, and now, Jennie was in his arms.

As Billy leaned over to kiss her, Jennie pushed him away. "Wait, Billy," she said. "Please. I don't feel good about being here."

"But we've both been looking forward to this time together!"

"I know, but I just don't like being up here alone. It's creepy."

"Come on," said Billy. "This is the first time I've been able to get my dad's car. It's going to be a long time before we get another chance like this."

"I know. But I feel scared up here. Really. I want to go."

"Why are you acting this way?" asked Billy. "Our first night alone together and now you want to leave?"

"It's just—I have a feeling something bad's going to happen if we stay here very long."

"Bad? What could be bad?"

"Oh, Billy, haven't you been watching the news? That crazy guy that escaped from Camarillo—the guy who has a hook for a hand? The guy who killed a couple in Oxnard with his metal hook? That's what's bad!"

"Jennie, we're fifty miles from Camarillo. You think some crazy guy with a hook is going to hike all the way up here to Mulholland Drive just to attack us? You're the one who's crazy."

"Crazy?" said Jennie. "Bad things happen all the time, Billy. Didn't you hear the story about that couple parked on Lover's Lane? It was a lonely place like this. They were parked underneath a big willow tree. When they decided to leave, he discovered the gas tank was empty. So he told her to stay in the car while he went to get some gas.

"She begged him not to leave her there by herself. She was scared. He reminded her that the gas station was a couple of miles back and that she wouldn't be able to walk that distance in her high heels. He told her to lie down in the back seat and pull a blanket over her head if she got scared.

"So he got out of the car and left. She lay down in the back and pulled the blanket over her head. During the night she was awakened several times by strange noises. She even imagined the sounds of someone screaming. Later on, she thought she heard a scraping sound on the top of the car.

"She didn't know what it was, and she certainly wasn't about to get up and see. Finally, she heard the sound of a siren getting closer and closer. As she stuck her head out from underneath the blanket, she saw a police car pull up. The cop got out of the car and came over. He looked in and told her to put the blanket over her head, get out of the car, and to not look back.

"The girl climbed out of the car, but her curiosity got the better of her. She turned around and looked. There, hanging upside down from a limb of the willow tree, was her boyfriend. It was his fingernails that had been scratching against the roof. The worst part was, he didn't have a head.

"Billy, that girl was so afraid, she never went out with a guy again."

"Aw, that's stupid," said Billy. "Just an old story. It's not true. It's the same kind of dumb story they say happened at UCLA. A girl comes back to her dorm room late one night. The lights are out and it's dark. While she's undressing and getting into bed, she hears her roommate humming. When she's in bed, she says, 'Goodnight,' but her roommate doesn't answer—just keeps on humming. Finally she can't stand it anymore and turns on the light by the bed. Her roommate's lying in the next bed, but her head's been cut off. And the humming keeps on. It's coming from somewhere in the room. Suddenly the closet door by the roommate's bed opens and there stands a man with a butcher knife in one hand and her roommate's head in the other."

"Why are you telling me such creepy things?" screamed Jennie. "You're scaring me to death, Billy. Take me home."

"I'm only trying to show you it's a story. Just a story."

"Billy, I'm scared. I don't want to stay here."

"Jennie, please, this is our one time with the car. I've been looking forward to this all week."

As he reached toward her, she said, "Billy, don't touch me! I've got a bad feeling about this. I want to go home."

Jennie folded her arms and glared at him. Finally, Billy said, "All right, we've always got to do things your way."

He slammed the car in gear, stomped on the gas pedal, and roared away.

"Billy, what was that sound?" said Jennie. "Like somebody screaming!"

"Oh, brother, there you go again. It was just the tires squealing."

"No, no, I thought I saw something moving in the dark there by the side of the car!"

"Jennie, your imagination is really working overtime tonight!"

During the drive back, the couple didn't speak. When they pulled up in front of her house, Billy sat with his arms folded, the car still running.

"Aren't you going to walk me to the front door?"

Billy got out, slamming the door angrily, and walked around behind the car. As he reached to open Jennie's door, he froze in horror. There, on the door handle, swinging back and forth, was a sharp metal hook—a hook that had been torn from the arm of the escaped maniac as Billy sped away.

High Beams in the Rearview Mirror

Millie got off late from work. She was tired and hungry, but it was too late to eat a big meal. She decided she would stop at an all-night convenience store and buy a candy bar and a soda. That should hold her until breakfast.

She pulled up in front of the store. Since she would only be gone a minute, she left the car running. After Millie purchased the candy and drink, she got back in her car and drove away. She noticed, however, another car pull out of the parking lot and move in right behind her car.

Millie didn't think much about it until she turned a corner, then another. It suddenly dawned on her that she was being followed. Millie knew this section of town well, so she began taking a circuitous route to her house. Each corner that she turned, the car behind her turned as well.

This couldn't be simple coincidence. As she neared her home, the driver of the car behind her put on the high beams and began flicking them. The glaring light reflected irritatingly in the rearview mirror. She raised her hand to shield her eyes and accelerated, hoping to lose him. No matter how fast she drove, the car behind her kept up the pace.

Millie was scared to stop at her home, since she lived alone. No one would be there to help her. She drove past her house. *What am I going to do?* she wondered. *Where can I go?*

She was within eight blocks of her best friend's house. She turned another corner and pressed down hard on the accelerator. The car behind her kept up the pace and its driver continued to flick the high beams at her. As she neared her friend's home, she could see that the lights were out. Were she and her husband asleep? What if no one was there? She didn't dare get out of the car and run up on the porch to knock. Driving on, she wondered where to go now.

The car following Millie stayed right behind her, the high beams flicking on and off at irregular intervals. *Where can I go?*

she thought. Then it occurred to her that the police station downtown was always open. There was bound to be someone there!

Millie's car skidded around a corner as she turned in the direction of the police station. She drove faster and faster, but the car behind her lost no ground, staying ten feet in back of her in spite of how fast or slow she drove. She hoped that a patrol car, cruising the neighborhood, would spot her car careering through the streets in a reckless manner. A speeding ticket was a small price to pay for police protection.

When she reached the police station, Millie dove out of her car and ran inside.

"Help! Help!" she yelled. "There's a man who's been following me in a car! He's outside right now!"

The police quickly surrounded the car parked directly behind Millie's. The driver continued to flick his high beams. The police opened his door and dragged him out.

"Wait!" the driver said. "I'm not the one you want. I've been following this woman because, right before she drove away from the convenience store, I saw a man get into the back seat of her car and lie down on the floor. She drove away too quickly for me to warn her. That's why I've been following her. I kept putting on my high beams to keep him from attacking her. Every time I saw him raise up behind her with what looked like a knotted cord to choke her with, I put on my high beams to distract him."

When the police opened the back door of Millie's car, there, crouched on the floorboard, was a man with a length of knotted cord in his hand.

The Vanishing Hitchhiker

Two Rutgers students, Brent and Dan, were going home for spring break. A little past six o'clock on a dark, foggy Wednesday evening, they began driving south on Route 130 toward their hometown of Haddonfield, Brent behind the wheel and Dan in the passenger seat.

As they drove along, the rain began to pelt down. Up ahead, through the fog, they saw a beautiful girl in a white dress standing by the side of the road. She was holding a newspaper over her head with one hand and motioning for a ride with the other.

"Gosh," Brent said, "she's gonna drown if we don't pick her up."

They stopped the car. Dan opened the back door and yelled out, "Hey, need a ride?"

The girl came running up, got into the back seat, and closed the door.

"Thanks so much for stopping. I really need to get home."

"Where do you live?" asked Brent.

"About five miles down the road. On New Street, first house on the left. If you could drop me off there, I really would appreciate it."

"What's your name?" asked Dan.

"Mary. Mary Smith."

"You look like you're about to freeze to death, Mary. Here, take my jacket and put it around you."

"Thanks," Mary said. "Thanks so much."

As they continued driving south down Route 130, the rain began to pelt down. The conversation slowed, then stopped. With the windshield wipers slapping back and forth, everyone stared straight ahead to make sure they didn't have an accident.

Suddenly, the rain let up.

"Boy, this storm is a real frog strangler," said Brent. "We anywhere near New Street yet?"

"The next corner at the stoplight," said Mary. "Just pull in and I'll hop out."

Brent turned the car to the right and stopped. Across the street was a nice-looking house with a big covered porch. Mary got out of the car.

"Thanks so much for the ride, guys. I really appreciate it."

Brent turned the car around, got back on Route 130, and started driving south again.

"Whoa, wait a minute," said Dan. "I forgot to get my jacket back from Mary. Turn around."

"Oh, come on, you can get it later, on our way back."

"No, man. I need it now. I'll freeze to death."

They drove back to New Street, got out of the car, walked up on the front porch, and knocked on the door. After a moment, an older woman opened the door.

"Excuse me," said Dan. "We gave Mary a lift home just now. I loaned her my jacket and I forgot to get it back from her. Would you mind asking her for it?"

A pained expression crossed the woman's face. She looked at both boys, then spoke. "My daughter, Mary, was killed in an automobile accident four years ago on this very day. Each year, on the anniversary of her death, somebody picks up her ghost and brings her back here."

The two students looked at each other, then back at her. "Get out of here!" Dan said.

"It's true."

"What are you talking about?"

"My daughter, Mary Smith, was killed in an automobile accident April 13, 1995."

"You kidding? She was as real as you or I. I mean, she was in the back seat shivering. That's why I loaned her my jacket. Now I've come to get it back."

"If you don't believe me, the graveyard is only six blocks away. I can tell you where Mary's gravestone is. You can go see for yourself."

The students walked back to the car.

"You believe this?"

"No, I don't believe it. It's weird. Why wouldn't she give me my jacket?"

"Want to check it out?"

"Naa, man, it's stupid. Let's get out of here."

As they got in the car they saw the newspaper Mary had left on the back seat. They picked up the paper and noticed the date: *April 13, 1995.*

They looked at each other, then drove to the graveyard in silence. They made their way through the gravemarkers until they found the one they were looking for:

IN LOVING MEMORY OF MARY SMITH
DIED APRIL 13, 1995

There, neatly folded, lying on the grave, was Dan's jacket.

The Belle of Biloxi

In 1960, Dolores graduated from high school in Biloxi, Mississippi. She was living on her own for the first time. She didn't have much money, but she made sure she budgeted enough to have her hair done professionally once every three months. She told Andre, the hairdresser down the street, that she wanted the latest style.

"Honey," he said, "have I got the hairdo for you! It's called the Beehive. It's all the rage now. The smartest women in America are wearing it. And here's the beauty of it: all you have to do to preserve it is spray it in the morning and wrap it up in toilet paper every night. It'll stay for months."

Andre ratted and teased her long black hair until it stood up in a beehive shape on top of her head.

Dolores knew she couldn't afford to have the beehive redone very often, so she followed Andre's instructions to the letter. She sprayed her hair every morning. Each night, she wrapped it in toilet paper and slept on her back so that she wouldn't mess it up. After several weeks of spraying and wrapping, her hair became like a helmet.

One morning, she awoke with a terrible pain in her arm. She looked down and saw a swelling with an angry red spot in the center of it. Terrified, she raced to the doctor.

"You've been bitten by a black widow spider," he said.

"It must have happened in my sleep," Dolores replied.

The doctor treated the bite. Three days later, she returned to the doctor's office with bites on both arms. The doctor immediately put her in the hospital.

"You can't be bitten many more times or you'll really be sick," he said. "You must have an infestation of black widows in your apartment."

When Dolores finally got well, she searched through her apartment. Spider webs were in every corner. She called in an exterminator to fumigate the place. That night, she felt safe and secure for the first time. But when Dolores awoke the next morning, the first thing that met her eyes were spider webs in every corner of the room.

How can this be? she wondered.

She called the exterminator and told him the spiders were back and their webs were all over the house.

"That's impossible," he replied. "I put enough poison in there to kill anything living."

"You've got to come back and spray again."

The exterminator agreed to return on Wednesday.

Tuesday morning, Dolores was awakened by a tickling sensation on her cheek. She opened her eyes and looked up. Spider webs stretched from her face to the bedstead, the lamp, and the pillows. In each web, she could see a black widow spider. As a shudder ran through her body, the spider webs began to shake and the spiders scrambled toward her face. She screamed and jumped out of bed. She looked back at her pillow, expecting to see the spiders. But there were none.

"Where did they go? Are they in my hair?"

Dolores ran to the bathroom and started unwrapping the toilet paper from around her head. Then she realized she was going to need help. *I can't do this alone,* she thought. She threw on her clothes and ran down the street to Andre's.

"Andre, you've got to help me."

"I can't," he said. "I'm sorry, but I've got a shop full of customers."

Dolores pulled a woman out of the salon chair and sat down. "There's something in my hair!" she screamed. "Get it out!"

As Andre began to unwrap the toilet paper, black widow spiders spilled out of Dolores's hair, down her shoulders, and onto his arms. Both of them began to scream.

Hundreds of black widow spiders dropped to the floor and started crawling around the shop. Andre's customers screamed in horror. The shop echoed with hysteria as Andre and the women raced to the door, black widows climbing up their legs.

Once everyone had pushed through the door, they looked back. Dolores was still inside. Andre and his customers watched in disbelief as she grabbed a pair of electric clippers and began to cut off her hair, down to the scalp. They watched as the beehive fell to the floor and burst open. Inside were millions of spider eggs, ready to hatch.

After she got out of the asylum, Dolores never let her hair grow back. From then on, she was known as The Bald-Headed Belle of Biloxi.

Father Knows Best

An American soldier, stationed in Bavaria, decided to attend mass one Sunday morning. As he seated himself in the last pew of the sanctuary, an usher came over, greeted him—"Wilkommen"—and gestured to him to follow. The soldier spoke no German, so he was unsure what was expected of him. He followed the usher up to the second pew, supposing it was customary for a guest to be seated up front.

The soldier didn't understand a word of the service. The mass was being celebrated in German rather than the Latin to which he was accustomed. Embarrassed, he resolved to do whatever the man seated in front of him did. When the man knelt, the soldier knelt. When the man prayed, the soldier prayed.

When the man in front of him suddenly stood, the soldier stood as well. At that, the congregation gasped and began to whisper among themselves. The soldier became rather confused and quickly sat down again.

After the service, a woman came over and asked him in English if he was aware of what he had just done. No, he said, he certainly wasn't. She told him that he had been attending an infant baptism. The priest had asked the father of the child to stand. The man sitting in front of the soldier happened to be the child's father and stood up. That is when the soldier also stood. So everyone thought both men were claiming to be the child's father.

The soldier was so embarrassed, he ducked his head and rushed out of the church. He was stationed in Bavaria for a couple of years, but he never attended mass again.

Just Add Water and Mix

A Latvian family moved to the United States and in time became reasonably successful. They continued to keep in touch with their relatives back in the old country and sent them many presents, including the latest American amenities.

Months passed without the family receiving anything. Finally, however, a package from the American relatives arrived in Latvia. There was no note attached, just a small jar filled with grey powder.

The Latvian relatives had become accustomed to getting packaged mixes from America—the kind that say, *Just add water, mix, and serve.*

The Latvians mixed up the sauce and ate it, but it was very gritty and really didn't taste good.

The next day, a letter arrived from America saying that Grandma had died and wanted her ashes scattered in Latvia. They hoped the letter would arrive before the package with the jar containing her ashes.

Putting on the Dog

A rich couple took their pampered toy poodle into a Vietnamese restaurant. The Vietnamese waiter, who had just arrived in America and did not speak English, approached their table and began gesturing toward their dog. The couple finally understood that he didn't want the dog in the restaurant and was telling them to take it outside. The rich people, however, were used to having their own way.

"No, no, dear fellow," said the man. "We're here to eat. *You* take the dog outside and walk it."

When the waiter did not seem to understand, the rich man reached in his pocket, pulled out a twenty dollar bill, and waved it under the waiter's nose. Then he handed him the dog and spoke slowly. "*You* go walk the dog. *Walk* it!"

The waiter finally seemed to understand. He smiled and said, "Ah ... *Wok!*"

He picked up the dog and left.

After a while, the waiter returned, carrying a covered platter. He ceremoniously lifted the lid.

There, perfectly cooked in a wok, was the rich couple's little toy poodle.

Scams and Conspiracy Theories

Losing in Las Vegas

Steve had a dream. He wanted to spend two magical weeks in Las Vegas. He had saved enough money to be able to gamble and not worry about the loss. He had enough to see all the new shows, eat well, and stay in the very best hotel.

Steve checked in and put on his best clothes. He looked sharp. Downstairs, shooting craps, he got lucky immediately. The management began sending him free drinks. People gathered to watch. Across the table, Steve noticed a gorgeous redhead.

This is the one, he thought. *But how to meet her? What line do I use? "Don't I know you from somewhere before?" "Didn't you go to my high school?" "What's your sign?"*

Then he remembered reading somewhere that women like honesty best of all.

Steve approached the redhead. "I don't usually do this," he said, "but you look so interesting. Do you mind if I talk to you? Buy you a drink?"

The woman smiled. Her eyes lit up.

As he talked to her, Steve realized they had a lot in common. They both loved the outdoors. They were both divorced and had no children. They each loved horses and dogs but hated broccoli.

"Let's go get dinner," he suggested.

"Oh, Steve," she said, "you're on such a wonderful roll. I hate to see you stop. Let me be your Lady Luck."

He won five hundred dollars—then a thousand, two thousand, three thousand.

"That's enough," said Steve. "We can buy the finest meal in town with this."

The conversation over dinner was relaxed and interesting. Steve felt as if he'd known this woman all his life.

After dinner, she said, "Why don't you come up to my hotel room?"

Just what he had been hoping for.

Once they were in her room, she began mixing drinks. "Steve, have you ever had a white zombie?" she asked.

"No," he replied, "but I'm willing to try anything."

She mixed the drinks. He drank his in one gulp.

The next thing Steve knew, he was waking up in a strange hotel room. The woman was gone. He had a terrible pain in his back. He saw a needle running from his arm to an IV stand. He couldn't understand what had happened to him.

Steve reached over, picked up the phone and dialed 911. He told the operator he was in a strange hotel and had an IV in his arm.

"Sir," she said, "slowly reach around behind you and see if you have a bandage on your back."

Steve reached behind him. Sure enough, it was there right above his hip. He said, "Yes, it's a gauze bandage, a big one, and my back hurts like crazy."

"Well, sir," said the emergency operator, "I'm afraid someone has stolen your kidney. You see there's a syndicate here in Las Vegas that's stealing kidneys and selling them overseas. You've been caught in a very clever and vicious scam."

It took a long time, but Steve finally recovered. These days, whenever he tries to pick up women, he no longer says, "I don't usually do this, but I'd like to meet you."

Now, just to be sure, his new opening line is, "Hi, my name is Steve, and guess what? I only have one kidney."

He doesn't get many dates, but at least he's still living.

The Diet Pill

You see all kinds of different diet plans: The Grapefruit Diet. The Slim-Fast Diet. The Protein Diet.

But did you hear about the company that put out a new diet pill? You could eat as much as you wanted without ever filling up and still lose three pounds a day.

Doctors around the country started getting concerned. When the pills were analyzed by the FDA, it was discovered they contained the heads of tapeworms. If you took the pills, the tapeworms started growing inside you.

The only way to get rid of the tapeworm was to fast for several days. Then the dieter was instructed to sit over a bowl of hot milk, holding his or her mouth open wide. The tapeworm, ravenous by this time, would smell the milk and start slithering up the dieter's throat. When the tapeworm stuck its head out of the dieter's mouth, the bowl would be pulled away a little. The tapeworm would inch out a little further to get a drink. The bowl would be moved again. The tapeworm would keep crawling toward the milk until it was completely out of the dieter's mouth. Then, the dieter could step on its head and kill it.

After that, those particular dieters decided they would just stay fat.

Light My Fire

A North Carolina man had a valuable collection of Cuban cigars which he had insured under his homeowner's policy. One night, however, he hosted a large, rowdy party, during which he proceeded to get drunk, break open his collection of cigars, and offer everyone a smoke.

The next day, when he realized what he had done, he called his insurance company and filed a report, claiming the cigars had "gone up in flame." The insurance company refused to pay, so he went to court claiming that his policy covered him for any "loss due to fire."

The jury ruled for the plaintiff, and the insurance company had to pay. But the insurance company had the last laugh. Two weeks later, the police showed up at the man's home and arrested him for arson.

The Everlasting Light Bulb

Back around 1930, a man bought light bulbs and put one of them in his kitchen. It seemed like an ordinary light bulb at the time. But almost seventy years later, it was still burning. The man was so impressed, he decided to write the manufacturers of the light bulb to tell them about their wonderful product.

He received a phone call from the manufacturer a week later. They were pleased the light bulb had given him such good service, but they would like to have it back. They were willing to pay $4,000 for it.

"Four thousand dollars for one light bulb?" the old man asked. "Why would you want to do that?"

They refused to tell him.

"In that case, I think I'll just hang on to it until you can give me a good answer."

By searching out every lead on the Internet, the man's son found out that seventy years earlier these manufacturers had patented an everlasting light bulb. When they realized the big profits were to be made by replacing burned-out bulbs, they had buried the patent and destroyed the light bulbs. But, somehow, one of the experimental bulbs got mixed up in an ordinary shipment and had lit the old man's kitchen for the past seventy years.

Attention K-Mart Shoppers!

Cathy dropped off her kids at soccer practice and drove over to K-Mart to buy a toothpaste, a hairbrush, and a comb.

She had just started searching for these items when an elderly woman walked up to her.

"Forgive me for being so familiar," the woman said, "but you look so much like my daughter. You see, I lost her in a boating accident four months ago. You look just like her. You even move like her. Would you mind if I walk with you a little bit? I'm so lonely for her."

Cathy was a kind person. "Of course," she replied, "I'd be happy to."

As the two made their way through the aisles, the woman shopped and put various items in her cart. Cathy picked up the few things she was looking for. The woman told Cathy all about her daughter and what a wonderful girl she had been. She asked Cathy about herself. Cathy told her she was a schoolteacher and showed her pictures of her family.

When they had finished their shopping, the woman entered the checkout line ahead of Cathy. As her purchases were being rung up, the woman turned to Cathy and said, "You know, I never got to say goodbye to my daughter. That hurts me so much. Would you mind terribly just stepping back and saying, 'Goodbye, Mama,' and giving me a big hug?"

Cathy found that rather strange, but the whole visit with the woman had been a little strange.

"Yes, of course," she said. "I'll be happy to do that."

Cathy stepped back, put out her arms and said "Goodbye, Mama." Then she moved forward and gave the woman a big hug.

"Oh, thank you so much, my dear," said the woman. "You're so kind."

Cathy was a little flustered as she glanced around at the people in line behind her. She turned back to see the woman pushing her cart out the door.

Cathy moved to the cash register and put her toothpaste,

hairbrush, and comb on the conveyor belt. The checkout clerk scanned them into the register.

"That'll be $357.49," the clerk said.

"No, no," said Cathy. "There must be some mistake. I just have these few things."

"Yes," said the cashier, "but your mother told me to put the TV on your bill."

Crime Doesn't Pay... Does It?

The Choking Dog

A friend of my uncle's has a beautiful German shepherd. Whenever she leaves her home, she always turns on the lights and lets the dog have the run of the house.

She had gone shopping one day and returned home to find her beloved dog lying on the floor, choking. The dog's tongue was starting to turn blue. She picked him up, put him in the car, and rushed to the veterinarian.

The vet told her he would have to do a tracheotomy, which involved running tubes into the dog's throat.

"This isn't something you want to watch," he said. "Go home. I'll call you as soon as I am done and let you know how he's doing."

The woman drove home feeling terrible about what her dog was going through. She hoped everything would be all right.

As she walked into her house, she heard the phone ringing. "Hello?"

"Thank goodness I caught you," said the vet. "Get out of your house immediately. I don't have time to explain, just leave right now and run to your neighbor's. I'll be over as soon as I can get there. I'm calling the police!"

She dropped the phone and ran across the street to her neighbor's house. The vet drove up the same moment as the police.

"When I opened up the dog," the vet told them, "I found three human fingers stuck in his throat. That's what was causing him to choke. There's got to be somebody in your house."

The police searched every room. They soon found the intruder—slumped in a closet, weak from the loss of blood.

Missing from his right hand were two fingers and a thumb.

The Cat in the Sack

Marge and Nancy planned to spend the whole day Christmas shopping. As they drove down Highway 74 toward the Midtown Mall, a tabby cat suddenly ran out in front of the car. Marge swerved, but the cat was caught under the wheels. She pulled over and stopped the car. As she got out and ran back, Marge saw the cat, lifeless by the side of the road. She looked around to see where the cat might live, but there were no houses along that stretch of road.

"I am sick about this," she told Nancy. "I can't leave this poor kittycat's body by the road."

"What are you going to do with it?" asked Nancy.

"Take it home and bury it. That's the least I can do. Let's look in the trunk and see what I can put it in."

Marge had bought a sweater for her daughter at Neiman Marcus a few days before. She took the sweater out of the Neiman Marcus shopping bag, wrapped the cat in the tissue paper, and put it in the bag.

"There. I'll take the poor thing home in this."

Marge returned the shopping bag to the trunk. Then the two women drove on to the mall. After spending several hours there, they decided to call it a day. Loaded down with packages, they walked back to the car.

Marge opened the trunk, took out the Neiman Marcus bag containing the remains of the cat, and put it carefully behind her. She and Nancy then bent over the trunk, arranging and rearranging the packages so that all their purchases would fit into it. When they turned around for the shopping bag containing the cat, it was gone.

They looked up and saw a woman walking briskly toward the mall, carrying the Neiman Marcus bag.

"She thinks she's stolen some valuable Christmas gift," Nancy said. "Let's follow her and see what happens."

Marge closed the trunk of the car. They followed the woman into the mall, staying far enough behind her to escape detection.

The woman made her way through the crowds, finally entering a restaurant. Marge and Nancy watched as she sat down and ordered. After the woman handed the menu back to the waiter and watched him walk away, she bent down, reached into the bag, and pulled the tissue paper aside.

Suddenly her eyes grew large. Astonished, she pulled the tissue paper back a little more, bent closer, then screamed, throwing herself backward in the chair. She fainted and slid to the floor.

The restaurant manager called the emergency squad. The paramedics rushed in with a stretcher and loaded her on it. As the woman was being carried away, her eyes fluttered open just in time to see Marge and Nancy pick up the Neiman Marcus shopping bag and put it on her stomach. "Here, dear," they said sweetly. "Don't forget your Christmas present."

Fowled Again

A pregnant woman was standing in the checkout line of a supermarket when she slumped over and fell to the floor. The manager rushed up and rolled her over to ascertain what was wrong. That's when he discovered she was not pregnant, just unaccustomed to temperature fluctuations. The bulge of her stomach was caused by a frozen turkey she was hiding under her coat. Stuffed in her ample brassiere were two frozen game hens.

The Stolen Purse

A widow, finishing her meal alone in a local restaurant, paid a visit to the ladies' room before driving home. Closing the door to the stall, she placed her purse on the floor and sat down.

Suddenly, a hand reached under the stall and grabbed the purse. The widow could hear footsteps running out the door. By the time she pulled herself together and emerged from the stall, the purse snatcher had vanished.

Distraught, she went to the restaurant manager, who in turn called the police. After they investigated the robbery, the police told her she had very little chance of her recovering her purse.

The moment she arrived home, her phone rang. It was someone from the restaurant telling her that her purse had been found and all the contents seemed to be intact. Would she like to come back and claim it?

At the restaurant, the widow was dumbfounded when the manager told her that he knew nothing about a phone call. No, the purse had not been recovered. Who could have called?

Mystified, she returned home again, only to discover that during her absence, her house had been broken into and all her valuables stolen.

The Matron's TV

A woman in a swanky Manhattan apartment opened her door to see a shabbily dressed man carrying a TV set.

"What are you doing?" she demanded.

The man stopped and said, "I'm from the TV repair shop. I got a call to pick up this TV set from your neighbor down the hall."

"Oh, great! Mine's broken too. Could you take another one in your truck?"

"Of course, ma'am. Glad to be of service."

The man was a thief. Neither TV set was ever recovered.

So Long and Farewell

A couple in St. Louis was having terrible marital problems. The husband had a ferocious temper. He was often away on business trips, sometimes three and four weeks at a stretch. When he returned home, he was always demanding and unreasonable.

The arguments between husband and wife began to escalate, finally becoming unbearable. The morning before the man was to leave on a three-week business trip, he told his wife to get out of his house! Leave! He never wanted to see her again!

When he returned three weeks later, he found the house completely torn up—furniture overturned, coffee poured on the carpet, books pulled from the selves, food rotting on the countertops, phone off the hook. It was a mess. He reached over, replaced the phone receiver, and began to clean up the place.

A month later the phone bill arrived, totalling $8,000.

The man called the phone company and said, "What are you doing to me? You sent me a phone bill for eight thousand dollars. It couldn't possibly be that much."

The representative for the phone company looked up his records. Yes, that was correct, she told him. Someone at that number had dialed the weather report in Sydney, Australia, and had been listening to it for the past three weeks.

The Stolen Wallet

A Wall Street trader took the subway to work one morning. On the train he was bumped hard by a man standing next to him. The trader was street-smart and immediately felt for his wallet.

It was gone.

The trader grabbed the man who had bumped him and shook him hard.

"Gimme that wallet!" he demanded.

The man was terrified and handed over a wallet.

When the trader got to his office he received a call from his wife.

"Honey, do you realize you left your wallet on the table this morning?"

The Note on the Windshield

A man drove to a shopping center. He spent an hour in a computer store trying out the latest models. When he returned to his car, he saw that the left fender was badly dented. A note was on the windshield.

> *The people who saw this happen and who are watching me right now think that I am writing down my name, address, phone number, the name of my insurance company, and my policy number. But guess what, I'm not. Sorry, dude. Better luck next time.*

The $100 Corvette

First thing every morning, a man showed up at the local newsstand and bought all the papers, thumbing through each one until he got to the classified ads. He wanted to make sure he was the first to find any good deals on used cars.

One morning, he saw an ad for a low-mileage Corvette priced at a hundred dollars. He couldn't believe his eyes. He was sure it was a mistake, but he decided to check it out anyway.

He drove to the address listed in the ad. A woman came to the door and said, "The Corvette is in the garage if you'd like to look at it."

It didn't take him long to realize the car was worth at least $25,000—maybe more. He went back to the house, took out a hundred-dollar bill and said, "I'll take it. But tell me one thing. Why in the world are you selling it so cheaply? You know it's worth a lot more than a hundred dollars."

"Well," she said, "my husband just ran off with his secretary to Las Vegas. They obviously gambled away everything they had. Then he had the nerve to send me a wire telling me to sell the Corvette and send him the money. But you know what? He didn't say anything about the price."

Keep On Truckin'!

Late one night, at a rest stop along I-40, a trucker stopped to get a cup of coffee and some food. He wasn't the big burly kind of trucker you often see—just a small, balding, middle-aged man. He had just been served his food when a motorcycle gang pulled up, parked, and swaggered inside.

No one else was in the truck stop but the owner and the truck driver when the bikers came in. One of the gang members started making fun of the truck driver while another one stuck his finger in the fellow's coffee. A third grabbed his sandwich and squeezed it between his fingers. A big fat biker stubbed out his cigarette in the trucker's french fries.

Obviously outnumbered, the trucker simply sat there and said nothing. Finally, he got up and, trying to avoid trouble, pushed his way through the bullies to the cash register. He paid his bill and, keeping his eyes to the ground, walked out the door.

Shortly after that, one of the motorcycle gang strutted over to the owner and said, "Ain't much of a man, is he?"

"No," said the owner. "Not much of a driver either. He just backed over twelve of your motorcycles."

The Big Shot

A friend of a friend of mine is a flight attendant for a major airline. She talked about a flight where she had to handle a particularly obnoxious first-class passenger. He complained about everything: the coffee was too hot; the food was too cold; his chair didn't recline far enough but the seat in front of him went back too far; he didn't like the wine list; and he had already seen the movie.

No matter what the flight attendant did for him, he disliked it. He let her know in no uncertain terms that he was not being treated as he expected to be. Nothing seemed to satisfy him.

Finally, with a withering look, he said, "Young lady, do you have any idea who I am?"

By that point, the flight attendant had given up being civil. She turned around, stood up on the adjacent seat, faced the back of the plane, and said in a loud voice, "Ladies and gentleman, we have a passenger here who has forgotten who he is. Does anybody know who the man in seat 2-C is?"

Have You Heard...?

Let Out at the Outlet

A woman was shopping in a coat factory outlet, a clearing house for inexpensive imported clothing. Although she tried on a number of coats, she couldn't find anything she liked and finally went home. Once there, she began to feel ill. She looked in a mirror and saw a large welt on her neck. She felt progressively worse. The worse she felt, the more it scared her. She drove to the hospital. The doctor in the emergency room informed her that she had been bitten by a snake.

"Where were you that you could have been bitten by a snake?"

"A snake?" she said. "There aren't any snakes out now. It's wintertime."

"Well, you've been bitten by a poisonous snake," the doctor said. "Fortunately, you came just in time. Where have you been?"

"The only place I've been is a coat factory outlet. I tried on a number of coats there."

Once she was treated, the woman returned to the coat factory outlet and asked to see the manager. He had the woman point out the coats she had tried on. When the manager looked at the coat racks he could see a subtle rippling motion, as if each coat were inhabited by an invisible specter. There, in the fur collars of the coats, were tiny poisonous snakes. They had been living in the coats imported from overseas.

The snakes had come over as eggs and, in the warmth of the store, had hatched.

The Theater Tickets

A couple kept a second car parked in front of their house and always left the keys under the floormat. One day they came home from work and saw an envelope under the windshield wiper. It contained a note:

Sorry, we had to take your car in an emergency. Please accept these theater tickets with our apologies.

—Your neighbors

The night the couple used the tickets, they returned to find their house stripped of everything.

Video Game Recruiter

You've seen electronic arcade games like Donkey Kong, Mortal Combat, and Space Invaders. At the end of each game, the machines record the total points and the initials of the highest scoring winners. You probably don't know, however, that these machines contain a hidden camera that takes your picture. The photo is combined with your initials and your score and reported to a secret government agency.

These games are actually sorting machines that find kids with the highest IQ and quickest response. These kids will eventually be recruited for secret military missions.

The Gas Pill

An inventor devised a pill that, when put into a tank of gasoline, would enable a car to get a hundred miles per gallon. The big oil companies found out about this invention and paid the inventor millions of dollars for the patent, which they promptly suppressed. The oil companies knew it would put them out of business if people were able to get their hands on those pills.

The Cactus

A friend of a friend of mine brought back a cactus that he dug up in the Arizona desert.

It grew and grew.

He noticed one day the cactus had grown appreciably more. In fact, it seemed to be swelling. He watched in amazement as the plant began to bulge and contract. Then it started trembling. As he stepped toward the cactus, it shook violently.

Suddenly, the cactus exploded.

Hundreds of baby tarantulas fell out and began crawling to every corner of the room.

Scooped

A few days after a raging forest fire had been extinguished, inspectors and rangers were tramping over the large burned-out area of the San Bernardino National Forest east of Los Angeles when they came upon the body of a man clad in scuba-diving gear, complete with tank, mask, wetsuit, and fins. No one could figure out what he was doing up there in the mountains until one smart soul remembered that the fire had been doused by aircraft scooping up gallons of sea water from the Pacific Ocean and dumping it on the fire. It appeared that the unfortunate scuba diver had been scooped up as well.

A group of society women came out of a theater matinee on Broadway. As they walked down the street, a car full of youngsters passed by. One of the youngsters pulled down his pants and mooned the women.

Outraged, the ladies decided to report the incident to a policeman. After they told him what had happened, he asked them where it had occurred.

"At the corner of Forty-sixth and Broadway."

"When did it occur?"

"It happened just moments ago."

"What did the perpetrator look like?"

"He was white and round and had a big crack right down the middle."

The Dangers of Urban Legends

A friend of a friend just told me this, so it has to be true. Apparently, a young man, after recovering from a snake bite while eating at McDonald's, awoke in a bathtub full of ice, feeling very sore. When he got up, he noticed that his kidneys had been stolen and saw a note on the mirror that said, "Call 911!" On his way to call 911, he realized that his computer had a virus that would destroy his hard drive if he opened an e-mail entitled "Join the crew!" The man was a computer programmer who was working on software to save us from Armageddon when the year 2000 rolls around and all the computers get together to distribute the $600 Neiman-Marcus cookie recipe, under the leadership of Bill Gates, who told me all of this in a mass e-mail last week, which also promised a free Disneyworld vacation and $5,000. The poor man then tried to call 911 from a pay phone and got jabbed with an HIV-infected needle in the coin return slot before seeing a note that said, *Welcome to the world of AIDS*. Finally, the wretch tried to drive himself to the hospital, saw a motorist with his lights off, flashed his lights at him then was shot as part of a gang initiation.

Further Resources

The most extensive collection of urban legends can be found on the Internet. Just specify "urban legends" in your search engine and prepare to spend hours wading through the selections.

BOOKS

Brunvand, Jan Harold. *The Baby Train.* New York: W.W. Norton & Co., 1993.

_____. *The Choking Doberman.* New York: W.W. Norton & Co., 1984.

_____. *Curses! Broiled Again!* New York: W.W. Norton & Co., 1989.

_____. *The Mexican Pet.* New York: W.W. Norton & Co., 1986.

_____. *The Vanishing Hitchhiker.* New York: W.W. Norton & Co., 1981.

Cohen, Daniel. *Southern Fried Rat & Other Gruesome Tales.* New York: M. Evans and Co., Inc., 1983.

de Vos, Gail. *Tales, Rumors, and Gossip: Exploring Contemporary Folk Literature in Grades 7-12*. Englewood, Colorado: Libraries Unlimited, Inc., 1996.

Smith, Paul. *The Book of Nastier Legends*. London: Routledge & Kegan Paul, 1986.

_____. *The Book of Nasty Legends*. London: Routledge & Kegan Paul, 1986.

Turner, Patricia A. *I Heard It through the Grapevine: Rumor in African-American Culture*. Berkeley and Los Angeles: University of California Press, 1993.

PERIODICALS

FoafTale News. Publication of The International Society of Contemporary Legend Research, Folklore and Language Archive, Memorial University of Newfoundland, St. John's, Newfoundland A1B 3X8 Canada.

Fortean Times: The Journal of Strange Phenomena. Distributed in the United States by Eastern News Distributors, Inc., 2020 Superior St., Sandusky, OH 44870.

Storyteller and musician DAVID HOLT is host of Public Radio International's "Riverwalk." His recording of Janell Cannon's best-selling children's book, *Stellaluna*, won a Grammy Award in 1997. BILL MOONEY starred for many years in the ABC daytime serial "All My Children" and is a two-time Emmy nominee for that role. Holt and Mooney previously collaborated on *Ready-to-Tell Tales* and *The Storyteller's Guide*. Their recording of *Spiders in the Hairdo* was nominated for a Grammy Award in the Best Spoken Word category.